SHOUTYKID is a great book... If you like *Diary of a Wimpy Kid* or *Tom Gates* you will like this book... it's really funny and it made me laugh.
Isaac, age 8

Unlike any book I've ever read. I loved it!
Sam, age 10

Awesome, epic, funny and entertaining. I love the way the book is written in the form of letters and emails and texts. I hope that the author writes lots more adventures for Harry.
William, age 9

SHOUTYKID

How Harry Riddles got nearly ALMOST FAMOUS

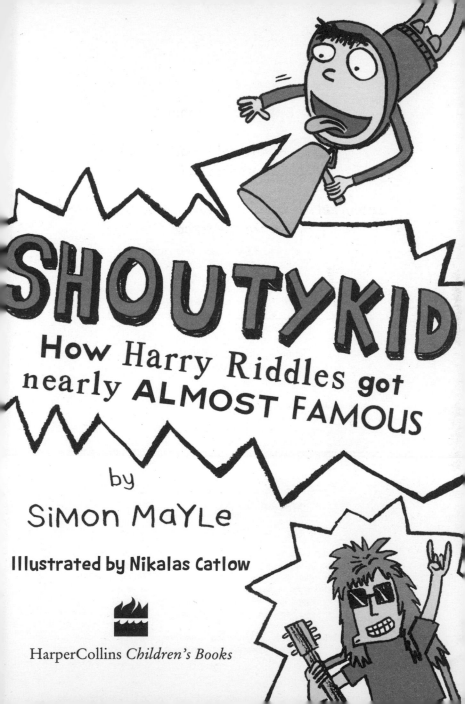

SHOUTYKID

How Harry Riddles got nearly ALMOST FAMOUS

by

Simon Mayle

Illustrated by Nikalas Catlow

HarperCollins *Children's Books*

First published in Great Britain by HarperCollins *Children's Books* 2015
HarperCollins *Children's Books* is a division of HarperCollins*Publishers* Ltd,
HarperCollins *Publishers*
1 London Bridge Street
London SE1 9GF

The HarperCollins *Children's Books* website address is
www.harpercollins.co.uk

1

SHOUTYKID – HOW HARRY RIDDLES GOT NEARLY
ALMOST FAMOUS
Text copyright © Simon Mayle 2015
Illustrations © Nikalas Catlow 2015

Simon Mayle and Nikalas Catlow assert the moral right to be
identified as the author and illustrator of this work.

ISBN 978-0-00-753190-5

Printed and bound in England by
Clays Ltd, St Ives plc

MIX
Paper from
responsible sources
FSC˚ C007454

This book is for my good friend and sailing partner,

Bruce Carr-Jones. With thanks and much love.

CHAPTER ONE
THE DROP SLIDE KID

From Harry Riddles **to** Charley Riddles
Subject: Aqualand
17 August 17:34 CEST

Dear Cuz –

Well, we made it down to Grandma's without getting lost, or missing the plane – which was pretty incredible considering Charlotte was in charge of everything.

Anyway, we're in Spain for like the next two weeks, which is gonna be great, cos Grandma always gives us lots of good stuff to eat. Plus, she spoils us rotten, so hanging out with her is Eee-Zee living!

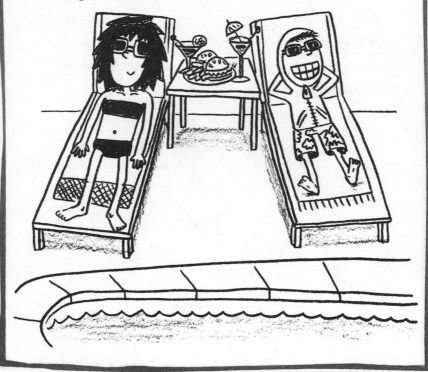

BTW, guess where we're going for our big holiday treat? AQUALAND! Yay! Grandma said cos Mum and Dad couldn't make it here this year, she's going to take us, which will be pretty INCREDIBLE, cos this park has got the biggest drop slide in the whole of Spain! And we're staying ALL DAY!!!

What's going on in California?

GBTM soon.

Yr cousin,

Harry

From Charley **to** Harry
Subject: Aqualand
22 August 11:26 PDT

Squid –

We're good. I got a summer job teaching
lacrosse to kids, which is cool, cos now
I've got like $900 saved for college, so I'm
psyched for September.

And BTW, that drop slide sounds sweet!
Don't forget your nappies!

Charley

From Harry **to** Charley
Subject: Drop slides
23 August 17:05 CEST

Why? I didn't say I was doing it.

What d'you mean you're not doing it?
Drop slides are FUN!!! U gotta do it!
Charley

But I'm too small!!
Harry

Says who?

Me

Harry – even your dog could do that drop
slide. So forget about not doing it and
man up, OK? Don't wimp out on me.

From Harry **to** Alan Eustace
26 August 19:21 CEST

Dear Alan Eustace, holder of
the world record for free-falling
from space, hi there!

I found this film on YouTube
where you got dropped from
the bottom of a BALLOON
135,000 feet above the earth
and basically free-fell for like
four minutes, breaking the
sound barrier on the way
down, before you opened your
parachute and landed in the
desert of New Mexico – which,
BTW, was a pretty AWESOME
thing to do and is why I think

you're the right guy to talk to about doing the drop slide at Aqualand.

I don't know if you've been on the Kamikaze before, but this slide is like really high and my sister says I'll never do it, cos I hate heights. Which is true. I do. That's why I need your help.

Do you have any great jumping-from-your-balloon-without-peeing-your-pants techniques? My sister said if I don't do the slide, she'll tell Jessica and every kid at my school that I'm a fail and Jessica should start dating somebody like Ed Bigstock, who wouldn't think twice about leaping off that slide, cos that kid's an idiot and would jump off Niagara Falls if Jessica asked.

So if you have any great advice for the pants thing, please write back to me soon. I don't want my sister messing everything up. OK? Thanks a lot!

Good luck and have fun.

Harry Riddles

BTW – if you ever want to play World of Zombies, my gamer tag is Kid Zombie and I'm online at weekends, plus Wednesday nights when I don't have any homework. So send me a friend request, and we can battle. OK? Cool!

From Charley **to** Harry
Subject: Aqualand
29 August 10:15 PDT

Smurf –

You have a good time at Aqualand? What happened? GBTM

Charley

_____

From Harry **to** Charley
30 August 18:51 CEST

Cuz –

OMG Aqualand was SO UNBELIEVABLE. But when we first got there Charlotte was like, "I'm not going on any rides with Harry! Harry's uncool!" So I'm like, "OK, well, if you're not gonna go with me, *who* is?" And Grandma goes, "*I'll* do the rides with you, Harry!"

So me and Grandma rent one of these big inflatable rafts and we hit the Rapids, the Boomerang and some other rides before Grandma says, "Harry – we have just GOT to do that drop slide!"

Well, I'm not so sure about that idea, cos that slide hadn't got any smaller since we arrived. In fact, I thought it looked even BIGGER. But my sister starts teasing me, telling me I'm a fail and a loser and all that other junk, so I'm like, "OK, we can go up there and take a quick look, but if I don't like it, we're coming STRAIGHT back down again."

So me and Grandma start climbing these stairs in the tower.

And we go up...

And up some more...

And then up again...

Until FINALLY we reach the top (and it's like REALLY high up there).

So I tell Grandma maybe we should just go back down and get some hot dogs. But Grandma doesn't want to go back down and eat hot dogs. Instead, she tells me about her good friend Hattie, who went SKYDIVING on her 90th birthday. She said if Hattie can jump out of an aeroplane twice in one day, then she can do the drop slide at

Aqualand. But she'll need some help getting on it.

So I help her over to the slide and we get one leg in, then the other, and just as she starts telling me about her amazing new hip replacement, some Spanish kids BUMP me and I FALL into her lap. Next thing I know, Grandma shouts, "We're off!" And before I can do anything, we're on our way...

OMG Cuz, I thought I was going to die. That drop was like so scary! But we BLAST down the slide, ROCKET on to the flat bit where

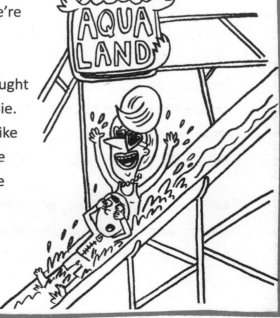

there's all this water to stop you, and when we finally climb out, I'm buzzing, cos I'd just done something I thought I could NEVER do.

Anyway, when we start walking away this park security guy comes racing over and starts yelling at Grandma, saying you can't take a kid on your lap on the Kamikaze, because it's too dangerous, and against park rules, and blah, blah, blah. So Grandma's like, OK. We're really sorry, sir. It won't happen again. But this guy won't leave Grandma alone, and as we head back to the pool area, he makes the BIG mistake of telling her she's an old woman and she really ought to know better.

Well, you can say all kinds of stuff to Grandma, but you don't call her old, cos that just makes her MAD. So she pushes the guy in the pool. Then she

dive-bombs him, which, BTW, was really funny. But
that was it for us and Aqualand, cos we got kicked
out.

But I didn't mind, cos Grandma's a heller and
I'm The Drop Slide Kid! What a GREAT summer
holiday!

CHAPTER TWO
BANDS AND BURGERS

World of ZOMBIES
COMMUNITY FORUM

31 August 19:28 BST

Kid Zombie: Walnut? You online?

Goofykinggrommet: Hey, Harry – welcome back! When did you get home?

Kid Zombie: Like ten minutes ago.

Goofykinggrommet: You have a good time?

Kid Zombie: Yeah. It was great. My grandma is hilarious.

 Goofykinggrommet: You do the drop slide?

 Kid Zombie: Uh-huh.

 Goofykinggrommet: How was it?

 Kid Zombie: Scary.

 Goofykinggrommet: Cool!

 Kid Zombie: What's going on here?

Goofykinggrommet: Not much.

 Kid Zombie: You been surfing?

 Goofykinggrommet: Yeah. Every day. In fact, right now I'm making a Batman suit for Wrongfest.

 Kid Zombie: What's Wrongfest?

 Goofykinggrommet: You know - the fancy dress surf competition we have every year at the beach for charity? There's a big party afterwards with bands and burgers and all that stuff. You should definitely come. It's gonna be great. Bring what'sherface.

Kid Zombie: You mean Jessica?

 Goofykinggrommet: Yeah. You still going out with her?

 Kid Zombie: I don't know. I hope so.

 Goofykinggrommet: I gotta go. Mum's calling. Welcome home, Harry.

 Kid Zombie: Thanks.

From Harry **to** Grandma
31 August 20:52 BST

Dear Grandma –

Thanks for having me and Charlotte to stay with you out in Spain. It was a GREAT holiday. Aqualand was the best bit, but I also liked going to Duffin Dagels to buy ice cream and use the Internet. I didn't like the mosquitoes, but I DID like the way you made Charlotte give me the window seat on the way home cos I'd let her use my suitcase for her extra junk, so thanks a lot for that.

BTW, did you find a necklace in my room? I bought it from that guy on the beach.

It's a really cool necklace with a shark's tooth on it and it was a present for my friend Jessica. So if you find it, can you send it, please? In fact, I've got a better idea. Why don't you just come and STAY with us, then you can bring it? The twins are driving me crazy cos they've now started crawling, which means you always have to keep an eye on them, or they disappear behind the sofa.

Plus, Charlotte's decided she now wants to be like Bob Geldof and save the world, AND be a famous pop star, which means giving everybody in our house an earful about recycling.

And, Mum says Dad's feeling kind of depressed, cos some skateboarder guy just died of a heart attack and he's my dad's age, so that's made Dad feel really OLD. So now he's got this running app on his phone and has started JOGGING, which I don't think Dingbat likes doing at ALL.

But if you came, you could take the dog out when I'm at school, then he wouldn't have to go jogging with Dad. Plus maybe you could cheer him up. So will you think about it? We miss you, Grandma. Come and stay soon.

Lotsa love,

Harry xxxxxxx

CHAPTER THREE
ROCK 'N' ROLL

From Harry **to** Charley
Subject: Kevin
01 September 19:42 BST

Dear Cuz –

Today was my first day back at school and I got to tell ALL my friends about doing the incredible drop slide at Aqualand – which, BTW, scored me a LOT of points even with that idiot Ed Bigstock, who said he didn't think a kid like me would EVER do that kind of thing. Well, I didn't either, but I didn't tell him about my grandma, cos he'd just say that was cheating. Anyway, the one person I REALLY wanted to tell was Jessica, but I didn't get to see her until after history, when her friend Becky Willoughby told me to go and meet her down in the music room.

So I go down there after class and I find a bunch of girls from Year 6, all standing around outside, and these girls are like, "Oh my God, Harry – have you heard this new kid, Kevin? He's like totally *incredible* on the guitar!"

So I go into the music room and I see Jess and I wave, but she's like way too busy watching this kid play his electric guitar, which, BTW, was unlike ANYTHING I've ever seen before, cos the kid was playing it with his TEETH.

Anyway, when he finishes, Jessica starts clapping and whistling, and I'm like, it wasn't THAT good. That was my first thought. My second was, I bet you don't do that in front of your dentist.

So then Jessica says, "Harry! Have you met Kevin?" But before I can get a word in, she starts telling me how Kevin's this really brilliant musician and songwriter who is probably going to be extremely famous, which would be great, cos nobody ever gets famous at Mount Joseph's. Then she says, "Kevin, meet Harry!"

So this kid takes off his guitar, and you know what the first thing he does is? Sticks his tongue out. Then he gives me the devil's horns with his two hands. Then he goes, "AAAAAAAAARRRRGH!" Right in my face. Which was really kind of annoying.

But I'm like, OK. Rock 'n' roll! So I stick my tongue out. Then I give him my devil's horns. Then I go, "AAAAAAAAAARRRRGH!" Right back in his face. But he gets mad, grabs hold of my tie and PEANUTS me!!!

(You know – when you yank the tie hard?)

Anyway, I push him off, he knocks his guitar over, one of the strings snaps and next thing I know, the kid wants to have a fight. And I only came in to listen to him play his guitar! So I leave the room and Jessica comes running out, telling me I should go back in and say sorry. I say why? She says because she and him are forming this new band to play in the local schools' Battle of the Bands contest at half term and if I was their drummer, we could hang out together.

From Charley **to** Harry
01 September 11:51 PDT

So ur in a band?

From Harry **to** Charley
01 September 19:59 BST

Nah. I didn't want to go back in the room.

From Charley **to** Harry
01 September 12:03 PDT

Why not?

From Harry **to** Charley
01 September 20:07 BST

Cos the kid's an idiot.

From Charley **to** Harry
01 September 12:09 PDT

So that's it?

From Harry **to** Charley
01 September 20:14 BST

I don't know. When we were waiting for my dad to pick me up, Jessica told me she thought I should make up with Kevin cos he was probably a musical genius, like Mozart. I didn't say anything, but I'll bet Mozart never went around peanuting people on his first day at his new school.

From Charley **to** Harry
01 September 12:16 PDT

U know what? Being in a band is cool. U should try it.

From Harry **to** Charley
01 September 20:18 BST

Why? I got better stuff to do.

From Charley **to** Harry
01 September 13:19 PDT

Like what?

From Harry **to** Charley
01 September 20:20 BST

Like shooting zillions and zillions of zombies!

From Charley **to** Harry
01 September 13:22 PDT

Heads up 4 u. Guys in bands r cool. Guys who shoot zombies aren't. Have a think about it.

From Harry **to** Charley
02 September 16:58

Cuz —

I had a think about it and you're probably right.

But my problem is, Kevin's definitely an idiot. Today in break Jessica brings him over to talk about the band and see if we can be friends. So I say hi and he says, "Hey, you know what this is, Harry?" And then he starts banging out some beat on my arm with his two hands. So I say, "Really annoying?"

He starts laughing. Then he tells Jessica how all the really great rock drummers in history – the Bonzo Bonhams, the Keith Moons, the Dave Grohls – they could all do these paradiddles, which is what he was doing on my arm. He says that's what they're gonna need from THEIR drummer if they're going to WIN this Battle of the Bands contest. So Jessica tells Kevin I could easily learn to do a paradiddle, cos I've been playing for a while. Plus if they had me, I could do other stuff too – like write to people who could help the band, cos I'm good at that.

Well, Kevin liked that idea A LOT. He said all new bands need to get their music out to their fans, and if he had somebody in the band that could do that, then that's one less job for him. So then Jessica says, "You can easily do that. Right, Harry?" and I say, "Sure." So he says, "OK. Come to the audition on Friday. Learn a Foo Fighters song – if you know who they are. "

Anyway, before I go, Bigstock comes racing over and asks Kevin if he needs a great rock singer for the band. Kevin says he has one: the beautiful Jessica Macdougal. Bigstock says we could always do with a better one: the amazing Ed Bigstock! So Kevin invites Bigstock along to the audition on Friday.

Well, that upset Jessica, but Kevin says he only told Bigstock he could audition to get rid of him. Jessica was his singer. AND his muse, cos she is just like he said: beautiful. Which made her laugh and me think that I've got to watch this kid, cos I think he's got his beady eye on her.

I thought you were already going out with her?
Charley

So did I.
Harry

So what happened?

I don't know. Just before maths, I asked her if we were going out and she said, "Where? Nando's?" So I guess we're not.

CHAPTER FOUR
THE BAND

From Harry **to** Charley
03 September 19:33 BST

Cuz –

I tried out for the band.

_____

From Charley **to** Harry
03 September 11:40 PDT

Cool. How did it go?

_____

From Harry **to** Charley
03 September 19:51 BST

OK.

From Charley **to** Harry
03 September 11:52 PDT

What's that mean?

From Harry **to** Charley
03 September 19:58 BST

Well, basically what happened was I'm on my way down to the music room when I run into Ed Bigstock and he's mad as hell about something. So I ask him what's up and he tells me Kevin's a mutant, his band sucks and he hasn't got a hope in hell of winning the Battle of the Bands contest. So I say, "Why's that, Ed?" He then tells me he's going to put together his OWN band with our music teacher Mrs Simmons's kid, Joe. He says Joe's a WAY better guitarist than Kevin will EVER be and that their band will annihilate

Kevin's. So I guess Kevin must have told Ed that he sucked, which is something Ed's not used to hearing, cos everybody always tells him he's great.

Anyway, I go into the music room and there's only me and McKenzie who have turned up for the drummer audition, cos most mums at Mount J's don't want their kids playing the drums. They prefer 'em to play the flute. Or the violin. Or anything that doesn't wake the dead when you play. But my mum loves rock, so in our house we play drums.

And when I told her I was going to try out for Kevin's band, she spent all Thursday night showing me how to play this cool Foo Fighters song, which was pretty awesome – until Charlotte came down and broke my sticks!

Anyway, I get to the audition and Kevin tells Jessica he wants her to wait outside, cos he needs to focus on my drumming and not her unbearable beauty (he actually said that). So we start playing and Kevin is the world's biggest show-off with his guitar, but he can really play. I only just manage to keep the beat without messing up, but when we get to the end, he doesn't say anything. So I don't know what to think.

Next he calls in McKenzie. But McKenzie is a human stork and WAY too big for the drum kit. Plus he's really lazy, so he doesn't bother adjusting anything. So when he gets to his first big solo, his long arms knock over the high hat, then the bass drum topples over, and basically the whole drum kit then kind of collapses. The kid even manages to fall off the stool, which is a pretty hard thing to do – unless you're McKenzie.

Well, this made things a lot easier for me, because basically drummers kick their drums over AFTER they've finished playing their set, not halfway through the first song. So Kevin tells me

I'm in the band, but he's putting me on a one-month trial – which was cool until he told Jessica the first song he was thinking of writing was going to be about *her*.

From Charley **to** Harry
03 September 12:00 PDT

Hey – you want to kick that idea into touch, PRONTO, buddy. You understand what I'm saying? Don't let this kid drop in on you. It's not cool, cuz. Got it?

From Harry **to** Charley
03 September 20:01 BST

Got it.

From Harry **to** Justin Bieber
06 September 09:15 BST

Dear Justin Bieber, pop legend and seller of
millions and millions of pop records, hi there!

Do you have to be a brat to be a good musician?
I'm in this band with this kid called Kevin, who is,
without doubt, the worst-behaved kid I've ever
met. Today he blocked up the
school toilets with loo paper
and they flooded, but
nobody except me
knows he did it.

Then he peanuted my friend Bulmer, cos Bulmer said Taylor Swift is cool and this kid HATES Taylor Swift. Then he disappeared for like an hour at lunch. And when he finally turned up late for French I asked where he'd been and he told me that school food sucks so he went out to Morrison's to buy a tuna fish sandwich.

Were you a toilet-blocker kind of kid? Did you sneak out of school during lunch break to get tuna fish sandwiches from Morrison's? Kevin says bad boys are what you have to be if you want to make it BIG in the pop business. And Kevin definitely wants to make it BIG.

He also told me all girls LOVE bad boys, which is why it's only a matter of time before my friend

Jessica will become his 'lady love' — that's what he called her. But I hope not, cos I like her too. You have any advice for that?

Please GBTM soon.

Good luck and have fun (but you probably are anyway).

Harry

HRH

HIS ROYAL HARRINESS

Tresinkum Farm
Cornwall PL36 0BH
7th September

Michael Eavis
Worthy Farm
Pilton
Shepton Mallet
Somerset
BA4 4BY

Dear Michael Eavis, holder of the greatest rock festival on Earth, hi there,

I'm in this new band with this kid, who told me that your festival is the number one place on the

planet that he wants our band to play. He said
if I could get us a gig playing at Glastonbury
next summer, I will definitely be the permanent
drummer for his band and not on a one-month
trial.

I'm not saying we should be on the Pyramid Stage, because we've only been playing for like a week, so we're not great. But by next summer we'll probably be able to play at least three covers without messing up AND have some of our own tunes written. So if you have a spare spot in the car park, how about we play there?

BTW, can we bring a snake? Kevin says a big snake would make us really stand out from all the other bands. Chances are, his mum won't buy him one, but if she does – can we bring it?

Plz GBTM soon, because I got a feeling me and Kevin are going to fall out, unless I can get us some gigs booked soon.

Good luck and have fun.

Harry Riddles

From Harry **to** Ezeld Trenneman
09 September 18:43 BST

Dear Ezeld Trenneman, organiser of The Kernow County 'Big Cheese' Cheese Festival, hi there!

You don't know me, but my dad met some guy in the pub last night, who said I should get in touch with you to see if you wanted a GREAT new band to come and play at your cheese festival next month.

We don't have a name yet, but our bandleader is a musical genius. If I give you my word that I'll keep him under control, will you think about giving us a slot in your line-up on the Saturday afternoon? My dad said The Fluid Druids and The Tankslappers have been booked, but you're looking for a few more good acts to play in the afternoon.

One last thing – can we bring Mr Slippy? He's a
9-foot boa constrictor that Kevin's mum just bought
for him as a divorce present. If we could bring him,

it would be really great, cos he makes us look cool on stage. Would that be possible?

Good luck and have fun.

Harry Riddles

From Ezeld Trenneman **to** Harry
10 September 15:13 BST

Dear Harry,

Thank you for contacting us and offering your services for a band slot on Saturday October 11th. Your father is absolutely right – we are looking for more acts, so please send me an audio file or a YouTube link of your band performing when you have learnt those songs and we'll see if your act will be suitable.

Unfortunately, we do not allow pet snakes on site, as they frighten our goats, so Mr Slippy will have to stay home.

We look forward to hearing from you soon.

Many thanks,
Ezeld Trenneman

CHAPTER FIVE
THE BIG TRIP

11 September 19:02 BST

 Kid Zombie: Walnut - you there?

 Goofykinggrommet: Hey Harry - wassup?

 Kid Zombie: I don't know. I think my dad's gone crazy.

 Goofykinggrommet: Whadya mean?

77

Kid Zombie: OK, so this evening I go up to the car park after band rehearsal – which, BTW, is not half as bad as I thought it was going to be – and Bigstock's dad is standing there next to his Land Rover waiting for Ed to come out of his band rehearsal. And up on the roof of his truck he's got this big red sled. So my dad's like, what's the deal with the sled, Ned? No snow on Dartmoor in September! But Bigstock's dad is like, "This is not a SLED, Wilson. This is a PULK!" So my dad says, "Looks like a sled to me!" But Bigstock's dad tells my dad that pulks may LOOK like sleds, but they are actually POLAR sleds, which is why they call them PULKS. And he's gonna drag his pulk all the way to the South Pole to raise money for global warming. So my dad's like, "Wow! You're really going to walk ALL the way to the Pole on your own? That's such a cool thing to do!"

Goofykinggrommet: What's so weird about that?

 Kid Zombie: It's not THAT. It's what he said AFTERWARDS.

 Goofykinggrommet: Which was?

 Kid Zombie: Bigstock's dad starts telling my dad how boring life is if you don't have some adventures. Every day the same old thing. Get up in the dark. Feed the kids. Do the school run. Same thing day after day, week after week, and then what happens? One day you don't wake up. Adventures, that's what keeps a man young! And my dad's like, "You know what, Ned? You're absolutely right! Maybe I need an adventure!" And I'm like, oh-oh. This doesn't sound good.

Goofykinggrommet: So?

 Kid Zombie: On the way home I tell my dad if his life is so boring, I could EASILY teach him how to play *World of Zombies* after school, cos that's lots of fun. Plus, if he got into it, we could break Mum's no-gaming-after-school curfew thing and play EVERY DAY!

 Goofykinggrommet: What did he say?

 Kid Zombie: He says, "I've got a better idea!" So I ask him what and he says, "We'll talk about it at dinner."

 Goofykinggrommet: So what was it?

Kid Zombie: I don't know - we haven't had dinner. But remember what happened the last time my dad got bored and wanted an adventure? He went paddleboarding and we had to get him rescued by the inshore lifeboat.

 Goofykinggrommet: Well maybe this time he'll build you a BMX pump track? And if he does I'm coming to live with you.

 Kid Zombie: I don't need a pump track. I just need to get some gigs for the band.

 Goofykinggrommet: So how's all that going?

 Kid Zombie: I got nothing confirmed yet, but Bigstock told me I should join his band and dump Kevin. He said Kevin's an Indy moron who thinks he's really cool, but isn't. And his music taste sucks, cos Black Veiled Brides and Slipknot are WAY better than the Arctic Monkeys – which is the kind of music Kevin likes. He also said if Kevin ever tries to peanut him again, it's gonna be war.

 Goofykinggrommet: So you gonna leave?

 Kid Zombie: No. Bigstock's just trying to use me to get at Kevin. And anyway it's kind of fun being in the band when we play good. Have you seen our video? I posted one of us playing on YouTube. You should check it out. We played two whole songs without messing anything up. It was really cool.

From Harry **to** Ellen MaCarthur
13 September 17:43 BST

Dear Dame Ellen MacArthur, England's greatest yacht woman and hero of my dad, hi there!

At dinner last night, my dad told us that he thinks it's time our family had a big adventure before he gets too old to go anywhere. My mum said she was definitely up for a big adventure – as long as there was a nice hotel and a warm swimming pool involved. But my dad said he wasn't thinking so much about a nice-hotel-and-warm-swimming-pool type of adventure, but more of a buying-a-sailing-boat-and-sailing-it-around-the-world type of big adventure.

Well I liked that idea a lot, but nobody else did. My sister told him we should be thinking about

SAVING the planet, not SAILING it, and my mum was like, "Why don't we just build an extension and then take a nice holiday?" And the twins just started throwing up.

So then my dad runs upstairs and fetches a pile of old sailing magazines he has stored in the attic. He lays them out on the kitchen table and tells us to feast our eyes on what life could be like if we went blue-water cruising as a family.

I'll tell you something. It was some feast. All these tropical bays with boats moored up – could be lots of fun, right? But neither my mum nor my sister were interested. My sister went up to her room to Skype Spencer and tell him about some protest she was thinking of organising at our local petrol station, and my mum took the twins off to clean them up before they got in the bath. So it was just

me and my Dad left at the kitchen table. He asked
me how I'd feel about doing something like this. I
said, "Do you even know how to sail, Pups?"
He said, "Kind of." I said, "What's that mean?"
He told me years ago he sailed a boat across the
Atlantic with some friends. They did some race.
But that was a long time ago and he didn't really
know what he was doing. He just did what they
told him to do – like pull this, try not to be sick
over that, don't let the big sails flap – that kind
of stuff. But he loved it and thinks this could be

a GREAT thing for us to do as a family, before everybody leaves home, or he gets too old.

I said, I think we're doing pretty good as a family. I mean, we still live in our house unlike some kids at my school who had to move school AND move house because of the recession. Plus, him and mum aren't divorced – which is a miracle according to Charlotte. So, we're like Grandma says: in a good place!

He said we could be in a BETTER place. And that place could be cruising through the South Sea Islands, where it's always hot and adventure is just over the next horizon. I said, "But if you don't know how to sail, Pups – how are we gonna GET to the next horizon?" He said he'll take a couple of courses at the local sailing club and then we'll be good to go!

Can you sail around the world if you do a couple of courses at the local sailing club? I know my dad can pretty much do anything, cos he's my dad, but I think maybe he's bitten off more than he can chew with this one. What do you think?

Plz GBTM soon.

Good luck and have fun.

Harry Riddles

BTW – I doubt you're the type of person who spends hours and hours gaming, but if you like *World of Zombies* and you need some help with your elite gaming prestiges, send me a friend request and I can help you out, cos I'm pretty good. My gamer tag is Kid Zombie. OK? Great!

CHAPTER SIX
GRANDMA

Grandma's coming!
Charlotte

Yay! When?
Harry

Mum thinks it might be today. And BTW – she's in yr room.

I don't mind! I love Grandma!

Grandma SNORES!

So do you.

From Harry **to** Charley
Subject: Grandma
19 September 21:40 BST

Dear Cuz –

Today me and Dad drove up to the airport to
pick up Grandma after school, but the first thing
Grandma said when she came through the gate
was, "My God, Wilson, you look *ill* – are you
feeling OK?" Which made my dad sigh, cos I guess
he thought Grandma was here to check up on him
and find out about this big sailing idea.

So we get in the car and Dad asks Grandma if
everything is OK out in Spain, cos we weren't
expecting a visit. Grandma says that after having
me and Charlotte to stay over the summer, she
realised that seeing all of us just once a year was

not enough. So she thought she'd get on a plane and come over, cos you never know what's coming at you around the corner. So my dad asks if she has a health problem. And Grandma says it's not HER health she's worried about, it's HIS.

So my dad starts sighing again. Then he says, "Please don't give me a hard time about the sailing thing. That's a long way off. And unless we get the girls interested, I don't think it's going to happen!" But Grandma starts to laugh and says, "But this is the best idea you've had in YEARS, Wilson! You have to go sailing!"

Well that cheered Dad up A LOT, cos finally SOMEBODY apart from me, thought going sailing might be a good idea. So then they start talking about the trip and how exciting it could be if he could only get Charlotte interested, cos if he could get Charlotte to come, then Mum would come too. He said the problem was Charlotte was only really interested in saving the world. So Grandma said, "Well maybe THAT'S how you get her to go sailing! Those Greenpeace people are always using their boats to try to save the world. If you tell Charlotte that's what you want to do, I'll bet you could get her to change her mind!"

So my dad said, "What do you think, Harry?"

I said, "If we could get Russell Brand to go sailing she'd definitely change her mind, cos she thinks he's hot. Otherwise, I doubt it."

Anyway, we've got our first dinghy lesson tomorrow, so I'll let you know what happens.

Harry

CHAPTER SEVEN
MID-LIFE CRISIS

20 September 20:21 BST

 Kid Zombie: Walnut?

 Goofykinggrommet: Hey, Harry. Did you go sailing?

 Kid Zombie: Yeah.

 Goofykinggrommet: How was it?

Kid Zombie: Great!

 Goofykinggrommet: Did Charlotte go?

 Kid Zombie: No. Just me, Dad and Grandma.

 Goofykinggrommet: Did you get your gran in a dinghy?

 Kid Zombie: Uh-huh.

 Goofykinggrommet: Did she like it?

 Kid Zombie: She said it was even more fun than getting kicked out of Aqualand. But I don't think the sailing instructor saw it that way.

Goofykinggrommet: How come?

 Kid Zombie: Cos she rammed him when the tiller got stuck in her life jacket. He capsized and fell in the water. It was pretty funny.

 Goofykinggrommet: Was he OK?

 Kid Zombie: Fine – until she asked if he was free for dinner.

 Goofykinggrommet: So is your dad still going through with this then?

 Kid Zombie: I don't know. Mum said we just have to let him think he's going to go through with it and eventually he'll drop the idea and go back to walking the dog. But I kind of want him to buy a boat, cos today was really good fun!

From: Vanessa@ellenmacarthurfoundation.org
to: harryriddles1@gmail.com
21 September 11:11 BST

Hi Harry,

Thank you for your email to Ellen. Ellen is travelling
a lot at the moment, so I am afraid she won't
be able to answer your email personally. I would
suggest you get as much information as possible
from the Royal Yachting Association. They are the
best people to help advise on safety issues and
courses.

Thanks and best wishes,

Vanessa Rom

From Harry **to** Vanessa
21 September 20:03 BST

Dear Vanessa,

Please tell Ellen things are moving pretty FAST in this house. Me, Dad and Grandma just did one day in the dinghies, which was really good fun for us (but probably not so much for the sailing instructor), so now we have another lesson booked for next month and we're hoping to get my mum and sister to come too. Plus, my dad has now signed up for a bunch of courses at the RYA, so thanks a lot for all your help.

Harry

From Harry **to** Charley
22 September 19:04 BST

Dear Cuz –

After school today Dad took me into Toy World,
cos he said he wanted to share this really cool
thing with me. So we go into the store and walk all
the way to the back where they have all the Star
Wars stuff. And I'm thinking – Great! A Millennium
Falcon! That's exactly what I need!

But Dad's not interested in the Falcon. Instead,
he points at this big globe that's standing next to
Chewbacca. He says, "What do you see, Harry?"
So I tell him I see the world.

My dad puts his finger down at Falmouth and says,
"OK. Now imagine my finger is our little boat. This

is where we're going to sail it."

So then I watched as he spun the globe slowly
around and the tip of his little finger traced a
route out across the Atlantic Ocean and down to
the Caribbean Sea. Then out through the islands
of the West Indies to the Panama Canal. Then off
into the Pacific and past the Cook Islands and on
to North Australia. Then up through Indonesia and
on to India.

And as I watched this finger travel across all those oceans and past all these little islands and places I'd never ever heard of I started thinking this probably isn't something we can get done in the summer holidays. So I ask Dad how long he thinks this boat trip will take. You know what he says? Maybe two years.

TWO YEARS!!!!!!!!!!!!!!

I spoke to Charlotte when we got home and she said Dad's having a mid-life crisis and this crisis could last between three and ten years for a man like him! So if it's not boats, it'll be something else. I'm just hoping that something else could be going back to walking Dingbat, cos as much as I like the idea of sailing, I don't want to go anywhere for two years.

From Charley **to** Harry
23 September 13:18 PDT

Ha! You only just worked that one out?!!

———————————————————

From Harry **to** Charley
23 September 21:20 BST

What?

———————————————————

From Charley **to** Harry
23 September 13:21 PDT

That it's gonna take years!

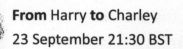

From Harry **to** Charley
23 September 21:30 BST

Well when I talked to Dad about it in the car on the way home, he said once we start sailing, and I get a taste for life at sea, I'll never want to stop. Swimming with dolphins, learning to dive with scuba tanks, walking up volcanoes on islands on the other side of the planet, meeting other kids who live on boats – it'll be a great way for me to grow up, instead of going to Mount Joseph's and playing video games all the time. I said I'm happy at Mount Joseph's. And I don't play video games all the time, cos you and Mum don't let me. Plus I'm in a band now, so I don't really need my life changing that much, cos I've got plans here. He asked me what plans could possibly be more EXCITING than doing something like this?

———————————————

From Charley **to** Harry
23 September 13:32 PDT

What did you say?

———————————————

From Harry **to** Charley
23 September 21:34 BST

I didn't. But us winning Battle of the Bands could be one thing. And going out with Jessica could definitely be another.

From Ezeld Trenneman **to** Harry
24 September 12:31 BST

Dear Harry,

Good news! We have listened to your two songs
and watched your video on YouTube and we think
you will be a really fun addition to our festival.
Please ask your dad to get in contact and we can
make some suitable arrangements.

Best wishes,

Ezeld

PS Don't forget what I said about Mr Slippy!!!

World of ZOMBIES
COMMUNITY FORUM

24 September 18:56 BST

 Kid Zombie: Walnut - you there?

 Goofykinggrommet: Hey, Harry - where have you been?

 Kid Zombie: Band practice. Drum practice. You know, busy, busy.

 Goofykinggrommet: Cool.

Kid Zombie: Who do I have to talk to to see if we can play at Wrongfest?

 Goofykinggrommet: Probably Crispin.

 Kid Zombie: I don't know him.

 Goofykinggrommet: I can ask him if you want. Did you ask at the skatepark?

 Kid Zombie: Yeah. They said send 'em a music file and maybe we can play at Fright Night.

 Goofykinggrommet: Cool. You want to do Map 22?

Kid Zombie: Can't.

 Goofykinggrommet: Why not?

 Kid Zombie: Cos I said I'd learn how to paradiddle before next band rehearsal.

 Goofykinggrommet: How's that going?

 Kid Zombie: I think Bigstock is getting scared we're gonna nail him in the contest, cos he keeps trying to get us kicked out of the music rehearsal room, but so far it hasn't worked. Anyway, Kevin said if he does, we can go over and rehearse at his house at weekends.

Goofykinggrommet: What about you and me and *World of Zombies*?

 Kid Zombie: I'm teaching Grandma to play, so when she gets better she can play with you. But I gotta practise. Battle of the Bands is not so far away.

1st gig cheese festival confirmed!! Also maybe Area 51 on Halloween!

Yay!

Harry

Jessica

From Kevin **to** Harry
Subject: Cheese Festival
25 September 19:20 BST

Harry

Fun addition'????!!! Who do they think we are?
Ant & Dec? I'll bet U2 or Coldplay never got told
they were a 'fun addition' when they headlined
Glastonbury!!!

Kevin

From Harry **to** Kevin
25 September 19:31 BST

Kevin,

It's a cheese festival. It's not Glastonbury. And we're not U2 or Coldplay.

CHAPTER NINE
SINGLE PRINGLE

From Harry **to** Charley
26 September 19:41 BST

Dear Cuz –

THE PIGS HAVE FLOWN!

From Charley **to** Harry
26 September 12:45 MDT

What are you talking about, Harry?

From Harry **to** Charley
26 September 19:52 BST

Me and Jessica.

From Charley **to** Harry
26 September 12:56 MDT

You and Jessica what?

From Harry **to** Charley
26 September 20:02 BST

I don't know if you remember, but Charlotte
said Farmer Harold's pigs will FLY before I get
the courage up to ask Jessica out again. But with
all this stuff going on with my dad and sailing
and Kevin, I didn't know how much time I've got
left. So all this weekend I spent going, do I? Or
do I not? What if I do and she says no? What if I
ask and she laughs in my face? What if Bigstock
finds out?

Then I thought maybe I could be like my friend
Bulmer and just keep asking and asking, until
eventually the girl HAS to say yes, just to stop me
from ASKING.

Or my friend Finley Quick, who writes a letter
to Poppy every day of the week and puts it in
her coat pocket in the locker room when she's
not looking, hoping one day she'll read his letter
and finally say yes.

Like Georgia Gardener said, "Do you want to be single Pringle, Harry? Or a taken bacon?" But when I get to school this morning, I see Kevin and he's like, how's the bandzoogle website build going, Harry? I tell him I'll need some band bios, then it'll be ready to post. So then he asks me about the contest admission and I tell him my mum has paid, so we're in. So then he tells me that him and Jessica are going to be spending a lot MORE time together doing songwriting stuff, cos we have to have one original song for the contest. But he won't need me for the writing part, cos I'm just the drummer — he's artist and Jessica is his inspiration.

Well that got my bells ringing LOUD AND CLEAR. I thought if I don't ask Jessica out now, Kevin definitely will. So I go and find Georgia and I tell her, "OK, this is it. This is the BIG DAY!" She says, "Are you going to ask her out?" And I say, "Yeah."

She says, "When?" I say, "During mid-morning break."

Which was a mistake, cos Georgia then runs off and tells EVERYBODY, so now the whole school knows what I'm going to do, which is a pretty scary thing.

From Charley **to** Harry
26 September 13:05 MDT

Lol.

From Harry **to** Charley
26 September 20:08 BST

In fact, the only people who DON'T know are the

teachers and Kevin, who got a detention for doing something.

But then just as I'm leaving English, Mr Jeffries says, "Good luck, Harry." So I ask him, "With what?" And he says, "With Jessica?" And I'm like, "Is there anybody in this school who DOESN'T know what I'm going to do?" And he's like, "I don't think so."

From Charley **to** Harry
26 September 13:15 MDT

As Vince Lombardi once said, "It's not whether you get knocked down, Harry. It's whether you get up!"

From Harry **to** Charley

26 September 20:21 BST

Yeah, well Vince Lombardi didn't go to Mount Joseph's. Or deal with being laughed at in the schoolyard when you make a moron of yourself. Anyway – who's Vince Lombardi?

From Charley **to** Harry

26 September 13:25 MDT

He won two Superbowls, five Championships, two Conference Championships. He knows all about achieving your dreams and not running away from a challenge. He was a great motivator and coach. My coach here in Denver LOVES this guy!

Well whatever. So I go out to the yard and every eyeball in school is now looking at me – including Mrs Williamson, who is head of catering. And she must have told the ladies in the kitchen, because they've ALL come outside the building and they NEVER come out the building during break unless it's to smoke.

From Charley **to** Harry
26 September 13:31 MDT

How much longer is this going to take,
Harry?

From Harry **to** Charley
26 September 20:36 BST

Not long. Anyway, I nearly didn't do it. But then
I see Jessica and I wave, but I don't go over, cos
I'm kind of having second thoughts. So Jessica
comes over with Georgia and she's like, "Is there
something you want to ask me, Harry?" And I'm
like, "Ah." And she's like, "Oh." And Georgia's like,
"C'mon, Harry – what are you waiting for? There's
never going to be a better time. ASK HER!" So I say,
"Jessica, will you go out with me, please?" And she

says, "I'd LOVE to go out with you, Harry!"

So that was that. I'd finally done it! (Again)

_____

From Charley **to** Harry
26 September 13:38 MDT

That's great, champ. What's next? Marriage?

_____

From Harry **to** Charley
26 September 20:40 BST

I'm too young. Besides Georgia then goes, "What
are you going to do now, Harry?" And I say,
"Can you give me a clue?" So Georgia says what
normally happens is, you hug the girl. So I say, "In
the middle of school break?" And Georgia's like,

"When else are you going to do it?"

So I give Jessica this big hug and I hear the ladies
from the kitchen start clapping, and now I'm
starting to relax and feel pretty good, but then

Bigstock comes running over and he shouts, "Don't tell me you two are going out!" And Jessica says, "Of course I'm going out with Harry!" Which felt great until Bigstock said he thought he was going to have to puke.

From Charley **to** Harry
26 September 13:44 MDT

Did he?

From Harry **to** Charley
26 September 20.45 BST

Nope. When Grandma came to pick me up, she asked me if I'd done it – cos I guess Charlotte must have told her. So I said I was now going out with the lead singer of our band! Grandma liked that. She told me that I was kind of like her old flame, Mick Fleetwood, who's the drummer with a band called Fleetwood Mac. She said he dated the singer of the band, who was some girl called Stevie Nicks.

From Charley **to** Harry
26 September 13:52 MDT

Grandma dated the drummer from Fleetwood
Mac??

From Harry **to** Charley
26 September 20:53 BST

That's what she said. But you can't trust
everything Grandma says, so I don't know.
Anyway, she said me and Jess were like Mick and
Stevie. A beautiful rock couple.

From Charley **to** Harry
27 September 13:54 MDT

Does Kevin know about you guys?

_____

From Harry **to** Charley
27 September 20:55 BST

Not yet.

_____

From Charley **to** Harry
27 September 13:56 MDT

Well, good luck when he does.

From Kevin **to** Harry
Subject: Band bio
28 September 20:31 BST

Harry,

Put this on our website. It's the band bio.

BIO:

"Kevin Williams is a musical genius who taught himself to play electric guitar before he could even talk. Currently Kevin has formed a brilliant partnership with the super talented and super beautiful Jessica MacDougal. Check listings below for their sell-out gigs."

What do you think?

From Harry **to** Kevin
28 September 20:59 BST

Shouldn't I be on it?

_____

From Kevin **to** Harry
28 September 21:01 BST

No.

CHAPTER TEN
LOST

From Harry **to** Bear Grylls
29 September 19:31 BST

Dear Bear Grylls, survival expert and Chief Scout,
hi there,

My dad's a big fan of yours and says he thinks all
parents should take a leaf or two out of your book
and get kids outdoors more. He says if kids had
dads like you, then they wouldn't drag their heels
when people like my dad want to take 'em sailing.

My dad has tried to make me and my sister more
outdoorsy. We've looked for buried treasure, built
a bird box, played Pooh Sticks, been to ball parks
and adventure playgrounds, gone on bat hunts.
We even went crabbing off the quay in the village.
But all of that is NOT as much fun as playing *World
of Zombies*. And maybe THAT'S why my dad thinks

sailing round the world would be a good thing for us to do.

But have you seen that movie *All is Lost*? That's one scary movie. It's about this guy who goes sailing his boat on his own somewhere, when he gets hit by this BIG storm. So he's like, OK, I can deal with this. But things just go from BAD to WORSE for him. And then from WORSE to YOU CAN'T GET MUCH WORSE, BUT I'LL BET IT DOES. And you know what? It DID. By the end of the movie, his boat has sunk and he's about to drown, when this hand reaches into the water and SAVES him.

Anyway, after we watched that film we were like, if that's what happens when you go sailing, you can count us out. But my dad says, "We're not going to get hit by a sunken container! That stuff only happens in the movies!!!"

But my sister said, what if we run aground on
a reef on some little island out in the Pacific?
What if we get shipwrecked and nobody knows
where we are, cos we haven't got a radio that
works, and we didn't tell anybody where we
were going? What if we end up on that island
like in that TV show, *LOST*?

I didn't see that show, but my sister has
watched the whole box set on DVD with
Spencer and she said the island's a nightmare
and we would need amazing survival skills to
get off it alive.

That's why I'm writing to you. Let's just say my
dad runs our boat aground on some coral reef in
some faraway place that has no people on

it (but hopefully lots of nice MONKEYS) – what
kind of stuff do I need to start learning to keep
this family ALIVE?

Plz GBTM soon cos I'm beginning to think my dad
isn't going to drop this sailing idea and go back to
walking the dog, cos he's just gone off to the boat

show in Southampton with Grandma and she's hardly what you might call a sensible influence.

Good luck and have fun.

Harry Riddles

From Crispin **to** Harry
Subject: Wrongfest
29 September 21:22 BST

Hi Harry –

Walnut said you wanted to play at our party. We
can fit you in at 4.30. But if you suck, we'll kick
you off.

Crispin

We can play Wrongfest, but it might be a tough crowd.
Harry

Come round to my house before and we can rehearse.
Kevin

CHAPTER ELEVEN
SILVER LINING

From Harry **to** www.bobgeldof.com/enquiries@
bobgeldof.com
30 September 19:44 BST

Dear Sir Bob Geldof, tireless charity worker and
organiser of hit charity singles, hi there,

Next weekend we have the Wrongfest fancy-dress
surf competition to raise money for Surfers Against
Sewage. This brilliant charity is trying to keep our
seas clean, so we don't end up throwing up every
time we go swimming at Polzeath beach (which,
BTW, has happened to me TWICE already this year).

Please can you come and be a judge at this
incredible contest? All you'll need to do is give
points to the person wearing the best outfit and
riding the biggest wave, and we'll make sure you
get on the local news.

If you'd like to try some surfing, Dan the Hobbit said he can give you free lessons. Plus, he will also throw in a board, a wetsuit AND one of his mum's world-famous pasties if you will give him a signed copy of your last great charity single (but he doesn't want that Boomtown Rats stuff).

And if you already know how to surf and you'd like to enter the contest, then that's OK, but you'll need to dress up. You can go as anybody you like as long as it's not the Pope, cos

that one's normally taken by Walnut's dad. But if he knew you wanted it, I'm sure we could make him go in as something else.

Will you think about it, please?

Good luck and have fun.

Harry Riddles

Did u really write to Bob Geldof?
Charlotte

Sure. And if he turns up you HAVE to come to sailing school. That was the deal, remember?
Harry

I thought you'd gone off the idea.

I have, but Dad hasn't and I don't want to drown.

From Harry **to** Charley
04 October 19:54 BST

Dear Cuz –

Today Grandma took me over to Kevin's house to have band practice before the Wrongfest gig, but Kevin lives MILES AWAY in a really HUMONGOUS house, so it took us forever to get there.

Anyway, when we arrive, they've got like four brand-new cars parked outside, but nobody is around. So we are just about to bang on the door when Kevin comes out with his bicycle and tells us he's cancelled band practice.

So Grandma's like, "Wait a minute. We've just driven over an hour to get here and you're cancelling band practice? Where's your mother?" Kevin says, "She's asleep." Grandma says, "At 11:30?" Kevin says his mum's always asleep cos she's depressed. So Grandma asks Kevin who keeps an eye on him if his mum's always asleep? Kevin says nobody because he can look after himself. He's a big kid. He's eleven.

So Grandma bangs on the door and Kevin says, "I can't believe you did that to me, Harry!" I say, "What?" He tells me drummers NEVER go out with the singers in the band – the GUITARIST does. It's an unwritten band rule. So I tell him, drummers DO go out with singers. Look at Mick Fleetwood and Stevie Nicks. They went out together, which means they never heard of that unwritten band rule. And these were guys who were in one of the biggest rock bands EVER. Much bigger than ours, so they'd *know*.

Well that stumped Kevin. So next he wants to know *how* I know about Mick Fleetwood and Grandma overhears him and says that *she* knew Mick Fleetwood, because she went on tour with him back in the 1960s. In fact, that tour *could* possibly be the reason why her grandson – me – is such a natural-born drummer!

Kevin didn't know what to make of that comment, and to be honest, neither did I. But I had a feeling that whatever it was, was going to be pretty embarrassing. Luckily Kevin's mum came to the door in her dressing gown and invited us inside but, Kevin was like, "I have to go meet Dad, Mum. Bye!" And before she could stop him, he got on his bike and took off.

So I run down the drive after him and remind him that we have our first gig later, but he cycled off, yelling that he had to go meet his dad. And that was that. I watched him disappear over a hill and thought, what am I going to tell Jessica and Crispin?

Anyway, I go in the house and Kevin's mum apologised and said this is not Kevin's fault, it's his dad's. His dad doesn't see Kevin much, so when he calls, Kevin drops everything and runs. Happens every time.

Anyway then Jessica arrives and she was like, "Where's Kevin?" So I explain and she's disappointed, but she says if he has to go and see his dad, then that's probably a good thing. We still have the cheese festival gig. And the Fright Night gig, which will give us plenty of time before Battle of the Bands. And maybe this cloud has a silver lining. So I say, "What's that?" And she says, "Wrongfest!" We should just forget about the gig and go boogie boarding. So that's what we did.

CHAPTER TWELVE
WRONGFEST

From Harry **to** Dear Deidre, Agony Aunt, the *Sun*
07 October 18:52 BST

Dear Deirdre,

I don't know if you remember me, but a while ago
I wrote to you and you sent me some stuff about
how to get over my shyness so I can start going out
with somebody at my school. Anyway, I read all that
and I think it might have helped, because I'm now
going out with that girl and you're probably the
only person apart from my mum who understands
what a big deal this is for me, so thanks a lot.

In fact, this weekend, me and her had our first
date. We went to the Wrongfest charity surf
competition. Have you ever been? It's really lots
of fun. What happened was, we got down to
the beach and all these surfers were changing

into fancy-dress stuff. One guy was dressed as a
butcher, another as an England footballer, two
surfers were dressed as old ladies, there was a
bumble bee, a spaceman, one guy had a shopping
cart on his long board, there were a couple of
sheiks, a pirate, a guy with a horse's head on,
some girls wearing pyjamas and another girl
dressed up as a barmaid. And you know what we
went dressed as? ZOMBIES! YAY!

Anyway, we didn't win, but after the contest we went up to the party in the field to see all the bands play and to apologise to this kid Crispin, because he had booked our band, but we couldn't make it, cos our guitarist had to go meet his dad.

So Crispin tells me and Jessica that's OK that we blew him out cos he found a really good replacement. And that's when we hear this kid we know, scream, "SHUT UP EVERYBODY! WE'RE FULL THROTTLE! WE'RE HERE TO ROCK!!!"

You know who the kid was? Ed Bigstock. And he's turned into this rock MONSTER – weird hair, make-up, fingerless gloves, a big belt with spikes, motorcycle boots. If I hadn't known it was him up there on the stage sticking his tongue out at everybody, I probably wouldn't have recognised him.

So we start listening and I was hoping he'd really suck and we wouldn't have any competition, but he and his band Full Throttle were pretty good – if you like metal music so LOUD it'll nearly burst your eardrums.

Anyway, that's why I think I might need some help. The kid who started our band got in trouble with the police at the weekend when his dad didn't show up. My grandma says he acts up all the time cos he wants attention. My problem is if this kid keeps getting in trouble, we won't have a band. Plus, he's now mad at me cos I'm dating his 'lady love'.

You have any leaflets for that?

Good luck and have fun.

Harry Riddles

CHAPTER THIRTEEN
LADY LOVE

Charley to Harry

What's going on with the band?
Charley

Just got ten times WORSE.
Harry

Kevin still mad at you?

No, Kevin's OK...

177

So what's wrong?

One guess.

Bigstock?

Uh-huh.

What did he do this time?

From Harry **to** Charley
09 October 20:59 BST

OK – so we were like just about to start rehearsing
when Ed barges into the music room with his band
and he's like, "OK, rehearsal time's over, losers!
From now on, Full Throttle has this music room
booked. You guys are in the broom closet down
the hall, ha ha!" So we're like, "What are you
talking about, Ed?"

So Ed gets Joe Simmons to explain that his mum,
Mrs Simmons, our music teacher, had told him
that he and Ed can use the room for band practice,
which is why we all have to leave. But then Ed
goes, "By the way, do you losers have a name for
your band? Because nobody at school knows who
you are."

So Kevin goes, "We have a name."

And – Bigstock's like, "OK – so what is it?"

Kevin tells Bigstock the name of our band is going to be Kevin. Bigstock goes, "That's it? *Kevin?* That's the dumbest name for a rock band I've EVER heard!" But Kevin just laughs. So Bigstock says he heard Kevin's parents were getting divorced. He says it's no big surprise given they have Kevin for a kid. What parent would want to live in a house with a son like him?

Well that did it. Kevin jumped on Bigstock and we had to pull him off, and now we're SWORN enemies with Full Throttle, and we're both going to be playing at the Cheese Festival, so it could be a Battle of the Bands before we even *get* to Battle of the Bands.

From Harry **to** Noel Gallagher
15 October 21:20 BST

Dear Noel Gallagher, godfather of Britpop and chief rival of some other Britpop band, hi there!

When I told my mum about the band beef we now have between our band and Full Throttle, she said we were kind of like you and Blur were back whenever it was. She said when you were in Oasis everybody in the whole country was talking about your beef with Blur.

That's kind of like what's going on at my school with us and this band Full Throttle. And now that we've been playing a while and we're really starting to click as a band. We even have three fans in Year 3 who wait outside the rehearsal room EVERY day. But this is making some members of our band even more obnoxious than they were already. Did you have that problem in Oasis? When you started to become really popular, one band member starts thinking they are God, and that everybody else is a moron? That's kind of what I've got to deal with and it's not easy.

For example, we were meant to have our first gig on Saturday at this cheese festival. The guy who is on in front of us is the lead singer for the Fluid Druids. His name is Kenny and he wears a suit and has a mohawk and glasses. Anyway, when the Druids finish their set, Kenny calls us up to come and play, but Kevin, our guitarist, has gone missing. So I go hunting around the fairground and eventually I find him over by the Portaloos. He has this big cheesy grin on his face and is looking like the cat that got the cream, so I ask him what he's doing by the Portaloos when we should be on stage. He tells me he's got Bigstock and Simmons, our main rivals, LOCKED in the loos.

Did you ever lock Damon Albarn in a Portaloo? Kevin didn't want to let Bigstock and Joe go, so we got in lots of trouble and just as I'm sitting

behind the drums to play
my first ever gig, we get
kicked out, because you
can't lock the other bands
in the loo. The only person
who thought this was funny
was my gran. She said if we carry
on behaving like this, we'll probably be really
successful.

But my mum told my gran that it was no laughing
matter. She couldn't tell Kevin off, cos he wasn't
her kid. Plus, Mum felt sorry for him cos nobody
from his family turned up to watch him play. She
said Kevin just needs some good parents and
he'll be a different kid. The thing is, I like making
music in a band, cos it's lots of fun. But Kevin is
probably more trouble than he's worth.

What do you think?

Plz GBTM soon.

Good luck and have fun.

Harry Riddles

CHAPTER FOURTEEN
PEACE

From Harry **to** Kailash Satyarthi
20 October 20:07 BST

Dear Kailash Satyarthi, winner of the Nobel Peace
Prize, hi there,

First off, congratulations for winning that brilliant
prize. We studied you in class and you are an
inspiration to everyone here at my school.
Hopefully my teachers will take a leaf out of your
book and change the child labour laws, cos we get
over one hour of homework every night, which I
think is TOO MUCH.

When you won the Nobel Peace Prize, it says you
got it for 'your struggle against the suppression
of children and young people...' Well, I have a kid
in my class who's going to get badly suppressed
if I can't get him some help. That's why I thought

I'd write to you.

Could you send a note to Ed Bigstock (ed.
bigstock@mountjosephs.co.uk) saying that you
are aware that he has plans to get even with
Kevin Williams (the kid I'm talking about) in
the schoolyard, cos of what happened in the
Portaloos, but you would STRONGLY advise against
it?

If he got a note from a guy who won the Nobel
Peace Prize, we might be in with a chance of
keeping Kevin in one piece before the Battle of the
Bands on November 5th. Failing that, how about a
quick letter to my mum (rita.riddles@gmail.com)
reminding her of Convention No. 182 and the
exploitation of child labour thing that you made
into law, cos I don't have enough hours in my
day to do homework, garden duty, walk the dog,

play with the twins, plus do all that other stuff
Mum wants me to do every day of the week,
AND still have time for band practice, band admin

AND shooting zombies with my grandma. But Mum said if I don't do it, I don't get my pocket money. Do you think that's fair? Or is she breaking Convention No. 182?

Please GBTM soon. Thanks a lot!

Good luck and have fun.

Harry Riddles

One last thing. I don't know if shooting zombies is allowed if you're a Nobel Peace Prize winner, but just in case you are, and you want to have some fun, I'm an expert at *World of Zombies* and I'd be happy to teach you how to slaughter the zombie masses.

BTW, my gran couldn't play when she first came to stay with us, but with my help and lots of practice, she's now well on her way to winning her second elite gaming prestige! So anything is possible.

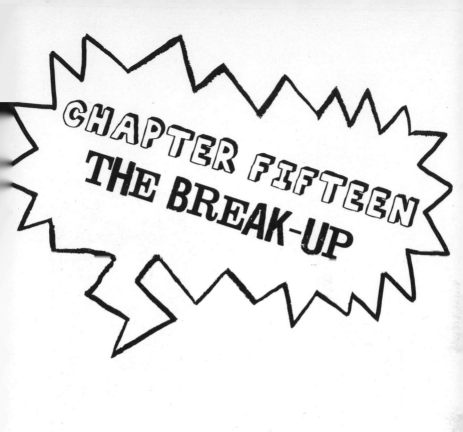

CHAPTER FIFTEEN
THE BREAK-UP

From Charley **to** Harry
26 October 09:10 MST

Squid –

OMG my college life is so GREAT! I don't
think I'm ever going to leave!

From Harry **to** Charley
26 October 16:14 GMT

Great.

From Charley **to** Harry
26 October 09:16 MST

U know why? I live in a dorm with sixteen

other freshman lacrosse recruits, 40 yards
from the field and weight room. Which means
I spend 30 hours a week, running, lifting and
practicing lacrosse. And only about 10 hours
a week in study hall!!

From Harry **to** Charley
26 October 16:19 GMT

Great.

From Charley **to** Harry
26 October 10:15 MST

Yeah. So in free time we have Xbox
tournaments, but the guys here prefer ice
hockey to *World of Zombies*. But if you lose,

you have to do a forfeit, which means running down to the girls' dorms two floors below and doing a stupid dare.

The only thing I miss is Dad's cooking and Mum's washing machine. Otherwise, I don't think I'm ever gonna leave.

From Harry **to** Charley
26 October 17:30 GMT

Great.

From Charley **to** Harry
26 October 10:32 MST

What's the matter with you?

From Harry **to** Charley
26 October 17:40 GMT

Nothing.

From Charley **to** Harry
26 October 10:43 MST

Is this about Jessica?

From Harry **to** Charley
26 October 17:48 GMT

No.

From Charley **to** Harry
26 October 10:52 MST

Don't tell me, u had ur 1st argument?

From Harry **to** Charley
26 October 17:54 GMT

OK, I won't.

From Charley **to** Harry
26 October 11:00 MST

What happened?

From Harry **to** Charley
26 October 18:03 GMT

U don't want to know.

From Charley **to** Harry
26 October 11:04 MST

I do want to know. I'm yr cousin. Maybe I can
help?

_____

From Harry **to** Charley
26 October 18:15 GMT

Basically, it was about sailing.

_____

From Charley **to** Harry
26 October 11:16 MST

OK. And?

From Harry **to** Charley

26 October 18:22 GMT

My dad said I'm gonna have to miss our gig at Area 51 at the weekend, cos we're having our second sailing lesson on the river. I said, why can't I just skip the course and go play at Area 51? I've finally found something I like doing that's not video games, but I can't do it, cos you want me to do something else. And I don't think that's fair.

From Charley **to** Harry

26 October 11:24 MST

What did he say?

From Harry **to** Charley
26 October 18:30 GMT

He said he was sorry, but once we went sailing I'd
see how great it was, and then I'd thank him for
making me do it. I said this is your thing, not mine,
Pups. But he said I have to go along cos it's an
important capsize recovery course. Plus, Charlotte
has now agreed to come with us (which, BTW, is a
BIG DEAL). I said, "How did that happen?" He said,
"Grandma." So I don't know what happened, but
Grandma must have said something.

_____

From Charley **to** Harry
26 October 11:31 MST

Hey – you'll only miss one show.

From Harry **to** Charley
26 October 18:38 GMT

One? This was going to be our FIRST and ONLY show before Battle of the Bands, so it's a big deal. When I told Kevin I couldn't play, he went nuts and yelled at Jessica that it was all HER fault that I was even in the band. So I said, "Wait a minute. Who got us kicked out of the cheese festival? Not me!" I said I really like being in the band, but if my dad wants me to do something else, I have to do it. He said if his dad asked him to do something and it got in the way of the band, he'd tell his dad to get lost. So I said, "Yeah? So why did you miss Wrongfest?"

So then Kevin kicked over a chair and stomped out the room. Jessica said I should have told them a long time ago that I couldn't play so they

could find somebody else. So I went and talked to McKenzie and said I'd help him learn my stuff if he wanted to play at Fright Night. He was psyched. But when I told Kevin that McKenzie could play for them, he said McKenzie was never going to learn how to play 4 songs in 3 days, so he's decided he needs a drummer he can rely on. And that kid's not me, so I'm out. And all because of stupid sailing.

From Charley **to** Harry
26 October 11:42 MST

The kid's a hot head. He'll cool off – but don't help McKenzie. You don't want him to be good. If he's good, he could take yr seat and then no Battle of the Bands for you.

From Harry **to** Charley
26 October 18:43 GMT

But I got to help him, cos I want to help Jessica.

From Charley **to** Harry
26 October 11:44 MST

Well don't say I didn't warn ya.

Tresinkum Farm

Cornwall PL36 0BH

27th October

Ozzy Osbourne

Mitch Schneider Organization

14724 Ventura Blvd.

Suite 500

Sherman Oaks, CA 91403

USA

Dear Ozzy Osbourne, Prince of Darkness, hi there!

My grandma said getting thrown out of a band doesn't necessarily mean it has to be forever.

She said look at you. When you and Geezer Butler made Black Sabbath back in 1969, you made a really cool rock band and recorded a couple of number one albums, before you got kicked out for being too crazy.

But then you went solo for like 31 years before triumphantly reuniting with the Sabs and recording the number one album, *13*!

Well, I just got thrown out of my band, but I don't want to wait 31 years to reunite. The truth is, I really want to play in the Battle of the Bands contest that's coming up. There's going to be like eight bands and the winner will be treated to a session at the world-famous Sawmills recording studios here in Golant, Cornwall (which is where The Stone Roses AND Oasis made their albums – so it's a really cool place). But first I have to get back in the band.

How do I do that if I haven't had a successful solo career like you? Normally I'd trade some elite gaming prestiges on *World of Zombies*, but Kevin doesn't play video games, cos he lives for music. So I don't know what to do. If you have any great ideas, please write back to me soon, cos this really sucks.

BTW, my gran says hello (but you probably won't remember her. Her name is Oona and she said she met you backstage at The Roundhouse in 1969).

Good luck and have fun.

Harry Riddles

CHAPTER SIXTEEN
JESSICA

From Jessica **to** Harry
27 October 18:24 GMT

Dear Harry,

Kevin has agreed to ask McKenzie to take your place
at Area 51, so don't feel too bad about letting us
down. It's a shame you won't be there, because
there's going to be a lot more people to watch
us than we had at the cheese festival and Kevin is
hoping he can get his dad to come and watch, so he
wants this to be the best show ever.

The only problem is Ed. He's found out we're
playing and says it's going to be payback time for
missing the cheese festival gig. Kevin says he's not
scared. But you know what? I think he is.

Anyway, have a good time sailing. I'll send a big

shout out to you after we play our first song, which, BTW, is going to be the new one that Kevin has just written.

Lots of love,

Jessica x

_____

From Harry **to** Jessica
27 October 18:29 GMT

Dear Jessica,

That's great. What's the song called?

From Jessica **to** Harry
27 October 18:31 GMT

Dear Harry,

It's not important.

From Harry **to** Jessica
27 October 18:32 GMT

Dear Jessica,

That's the title?

From Jessica **to** Harry
27 October 18.34 GMT

No, the title is, "Will You Go Out With Me, Dear Jessica?"

From Harry **to** Charley

27 October 19:01 GMT

Dear Cuz –

Jessica says it's OK to go sailing with my dad, cos
Kevin has now written her a beautiful song. The
song is about asking her to go out with him. My
sister said I should start listening to Taylor Swift
cos she's the break-up queen. And it's all because
of this dumb sailing thing. I wish we weren't going.

Tresinkum Farm
Cornwall PL36 0BH
28th October

The Duke and Duchess of Cambridge
Clarence House
London SW1A 1BA

Dear the Duke and Duchess of Cambridge, hi
there,

A while ago I wrote to you about giving my
sister a job as your au pair and a nice girl called
Claudia wrote back to me and said basically
you didn't want Charlotte looking after George,
which was probably smart, because my sister

has decided to save the world, so she won't have much time for babysitting.

Anyway, recently my grandma came over from Spain to stay with us, but now that she's been here a while, I'm beginning to worry that she might be a bad influence.

Does your gran come and stay with you and make your family do stuff you don't necessarily want to do? Mine is really keen that my dad buys a boat and takes us out of school to go sailing for a couple of years, but I think that's because she might want to come along too.

Is your gran like that? Does she like sailing or skydiving? My sister says my gran's bored and that's what happens with old people. They get restless.

If you have any great advice, please write back.

Good luck and have fun.

Harry Riddles

From Harry **to** Mick Fleetwood
Subject: My grandma
29 October 19:15 GMT

Dear Mick Fleetwood, founder of Fleetwood Mac
and one of the greatest rock drummers of all time,
hi there,

You don't know me, but you might remember
my gran. Her name is Oona Riddles and she said
she came touring with you back in the late 1960s
when you guys were just starting out.

My questions for you are:

1) Do you remember her? She's tall and has
    a big silver beehive and is really good fun
    (sometimes). She said you probably won't
    remember her, because you rock guys have

terrible memories. However, she has spent a lot of time telling me, my dad and my mum about what great times you all had on the road and how sad she is that you did not keep in touch after all these years.

2) Would you like to give her a call and invite her out to California for a visit?

My mum said if she got a call from you she'd be on the next plane out to

California, then my dad might drop this sailing idea and everything would go back to normal.

Please GBTM soon.

Good luck and have fun.

Harry Riddles

CHAPTER SEVENTEEN
WHAT HAPPENED IN PADSTOW

From Harry **to** Vladimir Putin
1 November 19:31 GMT

Dear Vladimir Putin, President of Russia, hi there,

You don't know me, but by now I'll bet you've heard of my sister. Please don't get too mad with her after what happened in Padstow. And don't feel you Russians are the ONLY ONES she picks on, cos you're not – she picks on ALL of us.

For example, every time I leave a light on now, she shouts at me to turn it off. And if I come home from school with some crisps, I can't bring the packet inside without her yelling about the waste. And if I'm running a bath, she'll scream at me to use the shower. And we shouldn't flush the toilets all the time. And we mustn't use the car when we can walk. And Dad and Mum should cycle everywhere (which is a stupid idea cos everybody drives at like 80 mph in Cornwall, so it's DANGEROUS).

And she's told my dad that he should get rid of our lawn, cos lawns are costly to maintain and are dangerous to our health and that of the surrounding wildlife. Which, BTW, is music to my dad's ears, cos he HATES mowing the grass and would much prefer to have Astroturf like they have in the NFL.

Which brings me back to my sister. The truth is, my dad was just trying to get her to take a sailing course with us, because he thought once she tried dinghy sailing, she might like it. Nobody for a minute imagined she'd sail across the river, board your Russian trawler, tie herself to the bow, then refuse to leave unless you stopped drilling for oil in the Arctic.

So I'm sorry your skipper missed the tide and had to wait for the police to come and untie my sister. But if it's any consolation, my dad will probably have to buy the sailing school a new dinghy, cos when she forgot to tie the dinghy up, the boat sailed off towards the Rumps and nobody has seen it since.

Good luck and have fun.

Harry Riddles

From Charley **to** Harry
02 November 09:03 MST

Little geek –

What's going on? You get back in the band?

From Harry **to** Charley
02 November 16:04 GMT

Nope.

From Charley **to** Harry
02 November 11:05 MST

How come?

From Harry **to** Charley
02 November 18:08 GMT

Cos I don't even know if there is a band any more.
Kevin didn't turn up for Fright Night. Jessica
waited all night, but he didn't show and didn't
call. Bigstock said it was cos he was chicken, cos
Full Throttle were also playing. But I just found
out from Spencer that Kevin, his mum and his
dad went for dinner on Halloween at this fancy
restaurant where Spencer works as a waiter. He
said Kevin got really
upset about something
and ran out halfway
through the meal, so I
don't know what's
going on with him.

From Jessica **to** Harry
Subject: Kevin
02 November 18:22 GMT

Dear Harry,

Kevin has just told me he's breaking up the band because his dad doesn't want him doing music any more. His dad said Kevin is wasting his time doing things that he thinks will be no use to him in the REAL WORLD. So I guess that's it for the band and the contest, which kind of breaks my heart. See you at school.

Love,

Jessica x

From Harry **to** Jessica
Subject: Kevin
02 November 20:25 GMT

Dear Jessica,

I hope you don't mind, but I didn't want you to feel upset, so I wrote to Kevin's dad. This is what I said.

Love,

Harry xxx

From Harry **to** Michael Williams
(michaelwilliams@venturecap.co.uk)
02 November 19:04 GMT

Dear Mr Williams,

I know I shouldn't be writing to you, because it's
probably none of my business, but I think you're
making a big mistake with Kevin.

The first time I saw him, there was a bunch of
girls from Year 6 standing outside the music
room and they were in AWE of Kevin's incredible
talent. They told me I had to go in and watch
him, cos he was amazing. So I went in the music
room and I wanted to hate him cos he's a real
show-off, but when I watched and listened it
really was something else. In fact, I'd say he could
probably play the guitar better with his TEETH

than most kids can play using their FINGERS.

Anyway, I'm not writing to you cos I'm his best friend. I'm not. In fact, me and him don't really get on. But I've never met a kid who loves something as much as he loves his music and if he quits the band now before Battle of the Bands, he won't get a chance to show everybody how good he is. Plus, he'll let my friend Jessica down and she's the singer.

So I guess what I'm trying to say is, you should give him a chance before you tell him to ditch his dreams. You might change your mind if you did.

Good luck and have fun.

Harry Riddles

CHAPTER EIGHTEEN
SHOW BOAT

Or that's it, we're stuffed. The Witch has woken!

From Harry **to** Charley
03 November 18:43 GMT

Dear Cuz –

OK, that's it. We're stuffed. The Witch Has Woken!

From Charley **to** Harry
03 November 11:50 MST

What are you talking about, Harry?

From Harry **to** Charley
03 November 19:01 GMT

Charlotte.

From Charley **to** Harry
03 November 12:04 MST

What about her?

From Harry **to** Charley
03 November 19:10 GMT

Now she WANTS to go sailing.

From Charley **to** Harry
03 November 12:12 MST

Around the world?

From Harry **to** Charley
03 November 19:13 GMT

Yeah.

From Charley **to** Harry
03 November 12:15 MST

How come?

From Harry **to** Charley
03 November 19:30 GMT

That protest thing she did with the Russian
trawler? Ever since she got on the front page of
The Western Morning Gazette, she's been a star
AND the most popular girl in her Politics and

Ethics class. So now she's told my dad that if she can get on the front page of the local newspaper using just a dinghy to get her message out, imagine what she could achieve if she was on a regular sailing boat!

She said she'd be more than willing to consider sailing with my dad, if we could make some of our journey link up with important work for Greenpeace, and my dad said we could do that. So Grandma then told Dad he'd better get that sea-trial organised, before she changes her mind.

Anyway, when Mum heard Dad had organised for all of us to go out for a daysail on the boat he was thinking of buying, the penny finally dropped that he was really about to go ahead and do this. So she kinda got hysterical and told Dad this has gone on too long and she does NOT want to go sailing ANYWHERE with him. And what about the twins? What happens if one of them gets ill when we're halfway across the Pacific? Then what do we do? So they had a big argument and my dad and my gran said she should just come out for the day and give it a try. She might really love it. So that's what

she's going to do. We're all going sailing for the
day over half term and if that goes well, I think my
dad will buy the boat.

From Charley **to** Harry
03 November 12:32 MST

That's great!

From Harry **to** Charley
03 November 19:40 GMT

For who? I don't want to go anywhere. I like being
at home. Plus, there's no Internet on the boat. It's
going to be worse than Spain.

From Charley **to** Harry
03 November 12:43 MST

What kinda boat?

From Harry **to** Charley
03 November 19:45 GMT

It's 40 feet long and was built in some yard in Korea. Dad said it's an amazing boat and we'll love it, but I think he's got blinkers on.

From Charley **to** Harry
03 November 12:47 MST

What do you mean?

From Harry **to** Charley
03 November 19:50 GMT

When I googled it, I read on this chat forum that
these Korean boats are 'show' boats, not 'go'
boats. So they look good, but they suck at sailing,
cos stuff breaks. That's why they don't cost more
than a new extension.

From Charley **to** Harry
03 November 12:52 MST

What did your dad say to that?

From Harry **to** Charley
03 November 19:54 GMT

He said the boat's perfect.

From Charley **to** Harry
03 November 12:55 MST

Well I guess you'll soon find out...

Dear Vanessa,

Thank you very much for asking for an update
on our round-the-world trip. The good news is –
WE'RE NOT GOING!!! We all went out for a daysail
on this boat my dad was thinking of buying and
the day was a complete DISASTER.

It started off OK cos it was a nice day when we left
Fowey. But things went downhill fast when my
dad took the wheel. First he accidentally gybed
the boat and the mast knocked my gran overboard
when she was trying to take some pictures of
dolphins. Then me and my sister fell in the water
trying to get my grandma out. Then my mum pulls

a muscle in her back trying to get us out. And
when we were all safely back on deck, the thing
that winds up the sails BREAKS. So when we finally
get down to Falmouth, we can't get the sail down.
So we try to start the motor, but that doesn't

start, so now the owner has to bring the boat into the harbour under sail power.

Well that didn't go too well either, cos he hit two other boats on the way in and then rammed the pontoon.

Luckily we didn't sink but it was a lot of stress and shouting and screaming and I guess my dad thought if we can have this much family drama in just two hours of sailing, how much more are we likely to have in two years? So he told the owner we're probably not quite ready as a family for a round-the-world trip.

Anyway, I don't think I'll need to be writing to you again, but thanks for all your help.

Good luck and have fun.

Harry

CHAPTER NINETEEN
BATTLE OF THE BANDS

Dear Jessica, I know we're not playing, but do you want to come with me anyway to watch

? Harry

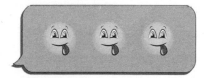

Jessica

257

258

From Charley **to** Harry
05 November 10:04 MST

Smurf –

What's going on? Did you kiss and make up
with Kevin? GBTM,

Charley

Nope. But in car now on the way to
Battle of the Bands!
Harry

U playing?
Charley

No, me and Jessica are going
to watch.

Cool.

Kevin to Harry

Messages

Clear

Where r u?
Kevin

At Battle of the Bands.
Harry

Come backstage.

Now?

Yeah. Where's
Jessica?

With me.

Bring her. U bring your drumsticks?

No.

Doesn't matter. Just get back here. Somebody wants to meet you.

From Harry **to** Charley
Subject: Battle of the Bands
06 November 17:20 GMT

Dear Cuz –

OMG, Battle of the Bands was awesome. You
know I said we weren't playing? Well, Kevin texts
me halfway through the show telling me to meet
him backstage. So me and Jessica go back and
we find Bigstock's dad with Full Throttle, and he's
talking to this other guy, who doesn't look like any
of the other parents backstage, cos he's wearing a
suit and tie.

Anyway, then I see Kevin's mum and she waves
to me and says, "Good luck!" And I say, "We're
not playing." And that's when I get a tap on my
shoulder and I turn round and there's Kevin with

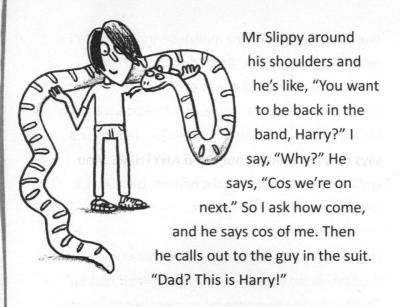

Mr Slippy around his shoulders and he's like, "You want to be back in the band, Harry?" I say, "Why?" He says, "Cos we're on next." So I ask how come, and he says cos of me. Then he calls out to the guy in the suit. "Dad? This is Harry!"

So Kevin's dad comes over and I think, oh-oh. But he says, "Are you the boy who emailed me?" So I nodded and he smiles and puts his hand on my shoulder and says, "Thank you, Harry."

Anyway, then I don't know what happened. There was like this mad panic, because we were due on stage in like two minutes. And we hadn't rehearsed for a week. And I didn't have any drumsticks. And we'd never even played in front of a crowd before. So I go and ask Bigstock if I can borrow some drumsticks, but he just laughs and says he's not lending our band ANYTHING. And we'd better leave the snake behind, because of health and safety regulations.

Luckily, Kevin's dad got one of the other bands to lend me some sticks, so now we're finally ready. The last thing I saw before we went out on stage was Bigstock taking Mr Slippy from Kevin's dad.

From Charley **to** Harry
06 November 10:23 MST

You win?

_____

From Harry **to** Charley
06 November 17:28 GMT

No. We had to do three cover songs and one
original, but we've never learnt our own song, so
we could only play the covers. But we played them
really well and when Kevin started playing with his
teeth, the crowd went NUTS. It was like the best
feeling ever. I wish it had gone on longer. But you
know what the funniest bit was?

From Charley **to** Harry
06 November 10:30 MST

What?

From Harry **to** Charley
06 November 17:31 GMT

Mr Slippy.

From Charley **to** Harry
06 November 10:33 MST

What about him?

From Harry **to** Charley
06 November 17:41 GMT

He tried to eat Bigstock!

_____

From Charley **to** Harry
06 November 10:44 MST

The snake tried to eat the opposition?

_____

From Harry **to** Charley
06 November 17:46 GMT

Yeah.

From Charley **to** Harry
06 November 10:46 MST

That's such a cool snake! I want one!

_____

From Harry **to** Charley
06 November 17:52 GMT

So that was Battle of the Bands. We didn't win, but we were Mount Joseph's top band in the contest. And Jessica even told me that it was probably the best night of her life, so that was all really cool. And you know what else? I think me and Kevin might end up being friends.

More to SHOUT about from *Harry Riddles*